JOUST OF HONOR

Also by Paul Stewart and Chris Riddell
A Knight's Story #1: *Lake of Skulls*

JOUST OF HONOR

A KNIGHT'S STORY

by Paul Stewart and Chris Riddell

SCHOLASTIC INC.

New York Toronto London Auckland Sydney
Mexico City New Delhi Hong Kong Buenos Aires

ISBN 0-439-80292-X

12 11 10 9 8 7 6 5 4 3 2 1   5 6 7 8 9 10/0

Printed in the U.S.A.   40

First Scholastic printing, September 2005

Book design by Tom Daly

The text for this book is set in Cheltenham.

The illustrations for this book are rendered in pen, brush, and ink.

For Anna and Jack

ONE

"I'm making you an offer, sir knight," said the duke, standing up to leave. "An offer you can't refuse."

"No," I said quietly. "I don't suppose I can."

As he left, I slumped back in my chair. He was a powerful duke, and I was a mere free lance. What choice did I have?

And to think, it had all looked so promising

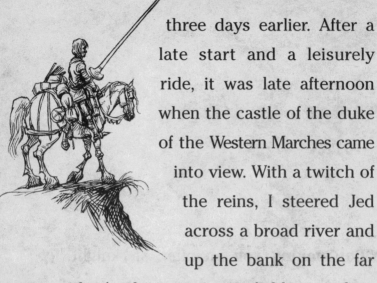

three days earlier. After a late start and a leisurely ride, it was late afternoon when the castle of the duke of the Western Marches came into view. With a twitch of the reins, I steered Jed across a broad river and up the bank on the far side. As the tournament field opened up before us, Jed pawed the ground.

"Easy, boy," I said.

I knew how he felt. Jed was a thorough-bred Arbuthnot gray. Jousting was in his blood, and it had been a long time since we'd seen a scene as magnificent as this.

"Welcome home, Jed," I whispered.

The tournament field was ablaze with color. There were pennants and banners,

tents and marquees. The air was charged
with loud voices and a tangy, mouth-
watering mixture of smells: leather,
manure, and a hog turning on a spit.

Yes, it felt good to be back at a major castle tournament.

I checked out the opposition. All the usual types were there: a boastful-looking customer—all swagger and confidence, with a snarling boar's-head crest; a rich, young nobleman with a fine tent, four squires, and a pack of white hounds—out for some excitement on the tournament field, while Daddy picked up the bill; and to my left, standing beside a particularly flashy marquee, a showman knight.

I had to laugh. With his baubles and tat, he was nothing if not eye-catching. Yet, judging by the tournament victories embroidered on his silk pennant, he certainly knew how to handle a lance.

Farther along, I came to a cluster of more modest tents belonging to the knights from the farmlands of the east. Big, stout petty-nobles, they were. Some were quite handy with a lance, it's

true—but to be
honest, they were
all far better suited to driving a plough.

Rich or poor, all the knights present had
one thing on their minds: the prize money.
The winner of the tournament would take
away a purse of fifty gold pieces.

Fifty gold pieces! That was more than

you could win in a whole year
of manor-house tournaments.

The place was packed.
Apart from the knights, there
were smithies and armorers,
merchants and servants, valets
and squires—and, no doubt, the pick-
pockets and other ne'er-do-wells who
never fail to appear at such gatherings,
where the cider flows freely
and the pickings are rich.

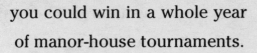

Close to the outer
castle walls were the
stables, where grooms
tended to the masters'
horses.

One of the horses—
a powerfully built black
warhorse—caught my

7

eye, and I wondered who might own such a fine-looking beast.

Probably the Rich Kid, I thought, and patted Jed on the neck. "Looks like you've got competition too," I said.

"You there!" cried a high-pitched voice. "Where do you think you're going?"

I turned to see a fussy-looking individual glaring back at me. He had red leggings, lace cuffs and collar, a tabard like a duchess's tablecloth, and a seriously bad haircut. Think of a fat black pudding boiled in goose fat and you'll get the idea.

"Are you talking to me?" I asked casually.

"I most certainly am," he squeaked, and flapped a piece of parchment at me. "Are you on the list? Have you wegistered?"

"Registered?" I said.

"I am the hewald," he said.

"Herald?" I said.

"If you wish to participate in the

jousting tournament, you must wegister with me. Dismount and pwesent yourself."

I'd seen his type before. Fussy little men who enjoyed ordering others around.

"I am a free lance," I told him, "up from the manor-house circuit."

The herald's top lip curled. "I'm afwaid you'll find a castle tournament much more taxing," he said. "You'll be up against the finest knights in the land." He looked me up and down. "I mean, are you quite sure you're good enough?"

Without saying a word, I reached inside my saddlebag. I was good enough, all right. I'd won my last five tournaments, giving me the right to mix it with the big boys—and here were the certificates to prove it.

"I think you'll find everything's in order," I said.

"Yes, yes," he said, thrusting the papers back at me. He pulled a piece of charcoal from behind his ear and entered my name at the bottom of his list.

Free Lance.

I tried to hide my grin from old Pudding Head, but it was no good. After all those years of village greens and run-down manor houses, I was back at the majors at last.

"Pitch your tent over there," said the herald, flapping a hand toward a thistle-strewn patch of grass beside the stable enclosure. It was far from ideal, but at least I'd be close to Jed. "The tournament starts at midday," he said, turning away and striding off.

11

I lit a fire, pitched my tent, and was soon sitting down to a supper of Squire's Stew—rabbit, snared at sunrise and stewed at sunset, with field mushrooms and wild herbs thrown in for good measure. This is the life, I thought.

All round me the bonded knights were being waited on hand and foot by their squires. Not that I was envious. Not for a moment. Along with the pampering came a lifetime of serving their masters. I'd tried it once, and knew it wasn't for me.

I am a free lance. My own man.

"Are you hiring, sir?" came a squeaky voice.

I looked up to see a lanky, flaxen-haired

youth with a big nose, a slack jaw, and freckles, standing in front of me. His tattered jerkin was stained with the remains of his last meal, which, from the look of it, had been eaten at least two days earlier.

"I'm not sure I can afford a fine squire like yourself," I said.

"I'm very cheap, sir," said the youth. "All I need is me keep—and a tenth share of any winnings, of course." He shrugged. "I've tried all the others, sir, but most of them just laughed. I'm a hard worker, though. I can polish your armor, groom your horse, and fetch firewood. I'm very good at fetching firewood. . . ."

Something told me I was going to regret this.

But then, the kid looked as though he could do with a break.

"All right," I said, "you're hired, if . . ."

"If, sir?"

"If you don't mind Squire's Stew."

"Oh, I love it, sir," he squeaked.

I handed him a plate. "What's your name, lad?"

"Wormrick," he said.

"Then tuck in, Wormrick. We've got a busy day tomorrow."

Just how busy, I found out soon enough. From the moment her lady-ship's silver handkerchief fluttered down from her snow-white fingers, Jed and I were at it nonstop.

A field-of-silver joust is a straight-forward affair. All you have to do is knock your opponent from the saddle. After a slow start Jed and I got into our stride, and knights, large and small, were soon dropping to the ground like bishops in buttered slippers.

The second day went even better. I pitched knight after fine, noble knight off their mounts, send-ing them flying to the ground. By now the crowd was getting excited. The bets were flying, and a lot of people were making a lot of money on yours truly.

But not me. I wouldn't see a brass penny unless I made it to the semifinals.

On the third day things got tougher. Now it was a gold handkerchief dropping from her ladyship's fingers that got the tournament underway.

A field-of-gold joust is one where, after the unseating, the knights engage in hand-to-hand combat until one or the other gives up. It can get pretty nasty, but the crowds love it.

I got the boastful customer with the snarling boar's-head crest in the first

round. He went down
hard, breaking his leg
in three places—
and wasn't boasting
anymore.

Next up was the
showman knight,
and I knew I
had trouble
on my
hands. I
unseated
him on our
first charge, but
he sprang back to
his feet like a fox-
hound with its
tail on fire. The
crowd roared as he set
about me with his broadsword.

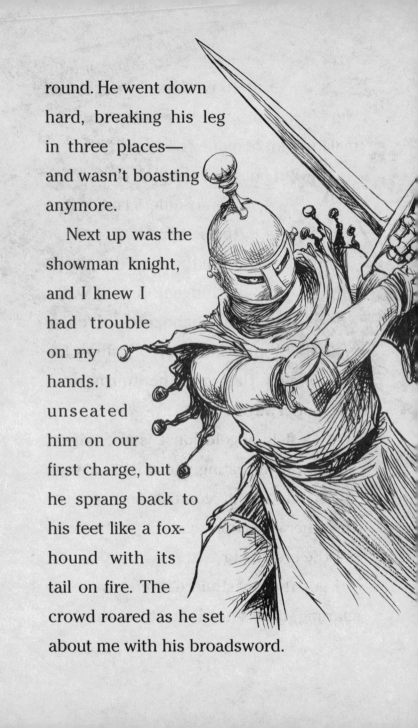

I bided my time, taking what he was dishing out, because I knew his sort. Can't resist playing to the crowd and trying one clever move too many. Sure enough, it wasn't long before Showman danced past me with a disguised right-hand slice—and I had him! A swift shield uppercut and a short, sharp body blow, and the show was over.

Later, back in my tent, Wormrick fussed about

my injuries. With a bit of
luck, there was nothing
that a bit of strapping
wouldn't see to. I
was through to the
semifinals and, as
Wormrick finished with
me and went off to see to Jed,
I pictured the opponent who awaited
me the next day.

Hengist was his name—
a great brute of a fellow,
bonded to the castle and
always clad in dull gray
armor. He was as hard
as nails and had a grim
reputation for fighting dirty.

In the other semifinal the
Rich Kid with the black warhorse had

made it through with a series of spectacular jousts. He was up against the Blue Knight, a mysterious character who kept his visor down and his thoughts to himself. He'd won through with a series of lucky victories, and nobody rated his chances highly.

Unlike me. All the smart money was being placed on yours truly winning outright. . . .

Just then the tent flaps opened and in walked the duke of the Western Marches himself. I'd seen him watching the events from the royal throne and noticed the glint in his eyes as he'd won bet after bet on my winning. Close up, he was fatter than I'd thought and, with his pointed yellow teeth and flapping ermine cloak, looked like nothing so much as an overfed wolfhound.

"You seem to be doing well," he barked. "People will make a lot of money if you defeat Hengist."

I nodded, taking his words as a compliment. I should have known better.

"But you're not going to do that," he said sharply.

"I'm not?" I said.

"No, you're going to lose," he said. His jagged teeth glinted in the lamplight. "But make sure you lose convincingly. No one must suspect a thing. . . ."

"And why would I do this?" I asked.

An unpleasant smile spread across Duke Wolfhound's fat face. "Here's thirty gold pieces for you now," he said, tossing me a sizable purse, "and there's thirty more later, when you've taken a tumble."

"And if I don't?" I said.

His yellow eyes narrowed. "Then I shall be forced to tell the herald that your documents are forged. You'll be thrown out on your ear." He sneered. "And don't think I wouldn't."

I didn't doubt it for a moment.

"I'm making you an offer, sir knight," said the duke, standing up to leave. "An offer you can't refuse."

"No," I said quietly. "I don't suppose I can."

So there I was, slumped in my chair, my head spinning.

Duke Wolfhound wanted me to throw the joust! Me, Free Lance, throw a joust! I'd never thrown a joust in my life!

Not that the offer wasn't tempting. I'd make more by losing the tournament than I would by winning it.

And as I was a free lance, that sort of money wasn't to be sniffed at. Then

again, there was the matter of honor.
Even if no one were to ever discover what
I had done, I would know. . . .

Just then the tent flaps
opened a second time, and
a tall, slim figure dressed
in a long, hooded cape
stepped in.

"We must speak at
once, sir knight," came
a voice—a woman's
voice. "It is a mat-
ter of the utmost
urgency."

TWO

Call me a fool, but I've always had a soft spot for a damsel in distress.

"How can I help?" I asked her.

"I . . . I hardly know where to begin," she faltered.

"You could start by lowering your hood," I suggested.

A snow-white hand emerged from a sleeve of her gown and pulled down the hood. A mass of auburn ringlets tumbled forward, and two dazzling emerald-green eyes fixed me in their tearful gaze.

It was her ladyship—the one who'd done the handkerchief dropping at the tournament. She looked as if she could do with a handkerchief now. I offered her mine, which she dabbed to her eyes and then held out to me.

"Keep it," I said. "Now, what's this all about? Shouldn't you be up at the castle prepar- ing for this evening's banquet?"

"Oh, sir knight," she cried. "You've got to help me! I beg you! You hold my future in your hands."

"I do?" I said.

"I followed my uncle here," she said. "I knew he was up to no good, and when I heard . . ."

Her face crumpled, and the tears began streaming down her face once more.

"Calm yourself, your ladyship," I said.

"I . . . I heard him make you an offer," she sobbed. "Promised you extra money if you threw the tournament. But you must not listen to him," she said urgently.

"No?" I said.

"I know my uncle," she said. "He's set this whole thing up. And it's not the first time. He holds a tournament, waits for a champion like yourself to appear—a champion who can't lose, who everyone has placed their bets on. Then he places

28

his money on the other knight—his man—and makes the champion an offer he can't refuse. . . ."

"His man?" I said.

Her ladyship shuddered. "Hengist," she said, her voice laced with disgust. "And what's more," she whispered, "if Hengist does win, . . . then . . . oh," she sobbed. "My uncle has promised him my hand in marriage. It doesn't matter that Hengist is brutal and cruel, only that he is loyal—and that I should be the reward for that loyalty."

"But what's this got to do with me?" I asked.

"Everything, brave sir knight!" she said.

I liked *brave*. She'd really gotten my attention now.

"I have come here to beg you not to

lose the joust tomorrow," she said. "If you defeat Hengist, and I know you can, then he will be disgraced in my uncle's eyes—and my uncle will punish him by calling off our marriage." She fluttered her eyelashes. "And you will have saved a helpless maiden from a fate worse than death."

I shrugged. "What's to stop him from marrying you off to another of his henchmen instead?" I asked.

"I won't allow that to happen," said her ladyship defiantly. "Even now, the one I love is planning our escape, an escape that will fail if Hengist gets his brutal hands on me tomorrow. So you see, I need your help," she said, "valiant sir knight, courageous sir knight. . . ."

She was certainly pressing all the

right buttons now, but
I was in a pretty
pickle and knew
it. If I were to
throw the joust,
then the beautiful girl
would end up married to
Hengist the Henchman.
If I didn't, the duke himself would be after me. I'd
find myself thrown out of
the tournament faster than a steaming
chamber pot from a bedroom window.

Thing is, I'm a sucker for a pretty face,
and they didn't come much prettier than
her ladyship's.

"Don't worry," I heard myself saying.
"Whatever happens tomorrow, I
give you my word as a knight that

Hengist won't lay a finger on you."

Her ladyship squeezed my hand. "I knew I could count on you, dear, sweet knight."

And with that, she turned and hurried away. I smiled after her stupidly, my promise ringing in my ears. What was I going to do tomorrow?

Just then Wormrick's matted hair and freckled face appeared at the tent flap. "The horses are all jittery, sir," he said, his voice high-pitched and breathless. "Something's spooked them."

"Rats, perhaps," I suggested. "Or maybe a snake. I'd better take a look. The last thing I need is something to happen to Jed, along with everything else."

"Everything else?" said Wormrick.

"You don't want to know, Wormrick," I said. "Come. To the stables."

The sound of troubled whinnying and neighing greeted us as we approached the makeshift stable enclosure. The horses had been spooked, all right.

As we approached, a tall, raven-haired beauty emerged from the shadows. She stopped when she saw us.

"I'm looking for my mistress," she said, fixing me with her dark eyes. "The lady of the castle."

"You won't find her in there," said Wormrick. "That's the stables."

Her ladyship's maid shot him a poisonous look.

"Your mistress has returned to the castle," I said. "Now, if you'll excuse us, I have a horse to attend to."

A flicker of a smile played on the maid's lips as she stepped back to let us pass.

In the stables the tethered horses were all skittering around, stamping their hooves and tossing their heads. The Rich Kid's black warhorse had broken out of its stall and was rearing up, pawing the air with its front legs. Its eyes were rolling, and glistening froth was dripping from the sides of its mouth.

I pushed past a squire, who was hopping about uselessly from one leg to the other, and approached the panic-stricken horse, arms wide and talking horsey sweet-nothings in a low, calm voice. The horse snorted and backed away, but I could tell by the way its ears twitched that it was paying attention.

"Easy, now," I murmured. "Nobody's going to hurt you."

Its eyes stopped rolling and, when I patted its neck, the horse turned and licked my hand. I've always had a way with horses. I only hoped Jed wasn't getting jealous.

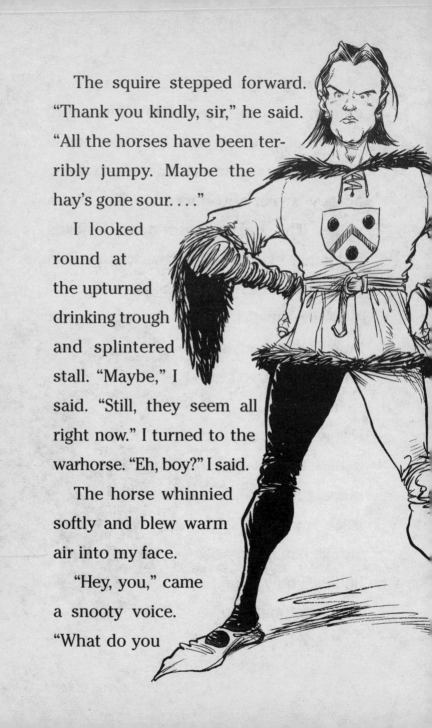

The squire stepped forward. "Thank you kindly, sir," he said. "All the horses have been terribly jumpy. Maybe the hay's gone sour. . . ."

I looked round at the upturned drinking trough and splintered stall. "Maybe," I said. "Still, they seem all right now." I turned to the warhorse. "Eh, boy?" I said.

The horse whinnied softly and blew warm air into my face.

"Hey, you," came a snooty voice. "What do you

think you're doing with my horse?"

I turned to find the Rich Kid standing before me, his hands on his hips. He was dressed in expensive-looking clothes, ready for the banquet no doubt. There was silver thread embroidered on his surcoat, and a ruby-encrusted gold buckle on his belt. The whole lot must have cost Daddy a pretty packet!

Our eyes met.

"What are you?" he sneered. "A squire? A serf?"

"He's a knight," said Wormrick indignantly. "And he just calmed your horse down. Why, the poor creature was in such a state it'd probably have broken its legs if he hadn't."

"Knight, eh?" said the Rich Kid, looking me up and down. "Sorry, old chap, didn't recognize you as a fellow knight. Still . . ." He eyed my patched tunic with evident distaste. "You've got to admit, it's an easy mistake to make."

I didn't rise to the bait—even though I sensed Wormrick would have enjoyed it if I had. The Rich Kid turned on his own squire.

"What have you to say for yourself, eh?"

"P-Please, sir," the terrified squire stammered. "One minute he was fine, the next I couldn't do a thing with him, and—"

"I don't have time

for all this now," the Rich Kid interrupted. "Some of us have banquets to go to."

"Yes . . . s-sorry, sir," said the squire.

"Rub him down and settle him in another stall," the Rich Kid called back as he strode to the door. "And if he gets troublesome again, take the whip to him."

I snorted. "Best way to ruin a good horse."

The Rich Kid spun round. "When I want your opinion, sir knight, I'll ask for it," he snapped. "Free lances," he muttered as he strode out. "Scum of the tournaments."

He was certainly pushing his luck, and under different circumstances I'd have taught him a lesson he wouldn't forget. But this was neither the time nor the place. Sometimes in my line of work a thick skin serves you far better than a quick temper. There would be time enough to teach him better manners on the jousting field.

I crossed the stable to where Jed was tethered. He seemed fine. I patted him, nuzzled my face against his, and told him he was the finest horse a knight could wish for. Wormrick came up behind me.

"When you've quite finished," he laughed, "Jed needs his supper. And you've got a banquet to go to, remember?"

"You're right, Wormrick," I said. I pulled some bits of straw from my hair, brushed myself down, and turned to face him. "How do I look?" I asked.

Wormrick grinned. "Not bad for a free lance," he said.

That was good enough for me. "Help

yourself to supper in the tent," I told him as I set off for the banquet. "And get a good night's sleep."

"I will, sir," squeaked Wormrick.

It was quite an honor to dine inside the castle itself, and I had made it to the semifinals—yet I felt none of the excitement and pride I'd expected to feel. Instead, as I clattered over the drawbridge, I couldn't get the sight of her ladyship's pleading emerald-green eyes out of my head, nor the sound of the duke's voice making me an offer I couldn't refuse.

THREE

I seized the heavy handles of the banquet hall doors and pushed them open. As I stepped inside, a blast of heat, noise, and smells struck me like a hammer blow.

The hall was tall and grand with ivy-decorated pillars; flags fluttering from the high, vaulted ceiling; and fresh straw upon the floor.

To my right a great fire was roaring.

I was late—that much was clear. All

round me, the banquet was in full swing, with the knights and squires at the long trestle tables, shouting loudly as they tucked into their bread and stew and supped their penny cider.

There were musicians in the gallery playing jolly reels. There were jugglers and tumblers and a character on stilts, all performing on the straw-covered floor and taking care not to step on the huge, gray-haired hounds that lounged about, gnawing on the mutton bones tossed to them by their masters.

Noisiest of all was the jester, a tiny fellow with bells on his hat and a voice more shrill than a princess caught on the privy. Leaping about astride a hobbyhorse, with a rough wooden sword in his hand, he was in the middle of some kind

of mock battle with a snappy terrier dressed like a dragon. . . . "Your name, sir?" came a voice, shouting above the din. I turned to see a page with a roll of parchment in his hands, looking me up and down sniffily.

"I'm probably on your list as Free Lance," I replied.

For a moment the page scanned the parchment. When he spotted my name, his eyebrows shot upward.

"Oh yes, indeed, sir," he said. "Follow me, sir."

I went with him between the rows of knights and squires, toward the high table at the far end of the hall. Some of them turned from their bread and stew and raised their tankards to me; others cheered.

"Fine jousting, sir knight!" someone cried, and the cheering grew rowdier.

I acknowledged their praise with a modest nod of my head, and noticed Duke Wolfhound eyeing me suspiciously. As the page led me up onto a low platform, I found myself standing before the duke. I bowed as ceremony demanded.

Duke Wolfhound—face flushed and fangs glinting—raised his goblet to me. "Eat, drink, and make merry, sir knight," he said. "You have an important day tomorrow."

I nodded. "Thank you, sir," I said. "Indeed I have."

The duke threw back his head and roared with laughter as if I had just told him the most hilarious joke.

To his left, Hengist—a huge leg of dripping lamb in his hand—leaned across and whispered something into the duke's ear, which made him laugh all the louder.

The page ushered me on toward my seat. As I passed her ladyship, seated to the duke's left, she stared at me, her emerald eyes welling with tears.

"Don't forget," she mouthed silently.

Forget? There was no chance of my forgetting what she'd told me. Not forgetting was easy. Deciding what to do about it was proving much more difficult.

I took my place. To my right was a matronly woman in dowdy clothes; beyond her, the Rich Kid. He was waving away a platter of meat like the spoiled brat that he was and demanding a flagon of their finest wine. I turned away in disgust. To my left was an empty seat.

"Who's meant to be sitting there?" I asked a page as he filled my tankard with thick two-penny cider.

"The Blue Knight, sir," he replied. "But he's been keeping to himself all tournament."

I nodded. Given the Blue Knight's dismal jousting skills, I wasn't surprised that he'd hit on the gimmick of being mysterious to keep the crowds interested. He'd had some really lucky victories—opponents' horses bolting or throwing their riders. Then again, you get those in any tournament, and fluke or no fluke, he had ended up in the semifinals.

"What would sir care to start with?" came a voice as a second page appeared at my shoulder.

There were salmon and trout, pâtés and truffles, and quivering molds of larks' tongues in aspic. . . .

"I think I'll try a little bit of everything," I said.

The two pages leaped into action. I tucked in. Everything tasted even better than it looked—apart from the jellied larks' tongues, which I threw to the dogs.

The second course was even more spectacular: suckling pigs with apples in their mouths, roasted peacocks dressed in their own feathers, capons and pheasants, and silver platters of sliced meats, dripping with sauces. The pages saw to my every need, slicing and serving and never allowing my tankard to get less than half-full.

I would have preferred to eat in silence, but the matron to my right—an aunt of the duke as I soon discovered—was having none of it. She talked of the weather, of the seasons, of her relatives, of prayer and duty, of the freshness of the straw and the brightness of the candles—not to mention the second-rate jester.

"His perform-ance is so boring."

She yawned. "We've seen this George-and-the-Dragon business so many times before."

I nodded, but made no reply. She didn't seem to notice and kept on talking—her theme now the colors of the flags hanging above our heads, and how red did so clash with green.

I looked round. The Rich Kid was tossing lumps of meat to his white hounds. Hengist and Duke Wolfhound were deep in conversation. Her ladyship sat staring straight ahead of her, not touching the food laid before her by her raven-haired handmaid. When two of the white wolfhounds got into a vicious fight over a scrap of meat, the handmaid looked over at the Rich Kid as he struggled to part them, a look of unpleasant amusement on her face.

"Ah, now this is more like it," said the matron, nudging me in the ribs. "The troubadour."

I turned round to see a tall, young fellow dressed in simple clothes, striding to the front of the minstrel gallery and strumming his lute.

The revelers fell still. The troubadour burst into song.

"My lords and ladies, listen well," he sang, his voice—like all troubadours' voices, so far as I am concerned—too high-pitched, like a knight in tight leggings. He made his way down the stairs. "I have a chivalrous tale to tell . . ."

Beside me the matron
sighed longingly and
closed her eyes.
The knights at
the low tables
seemed equally
spellbound. For
my part I'd heard
it all before—endless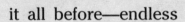
tales of sweet damsels and wicked
villains, and a knight in shining armor
who arrives to put everything right.

Life just wasn't that simple. And I
should know—even though there were
some who believed that it was, I thought,
turning to look at her ladyship.

Her expression took me by surprise.
She was looking up, her unblinking gaze
staring at the troubadour as he crossed

the hall. Her face was radiant—
her lips softly parted and
eyes gleaming with
excitement.

So that's her
loved one! I
groaned. If she
was in love
with a trouba-
dour, then she was
in more trouble than I thought.

I continued my meal, deep in thought.
Her ladyship had been promised to a
great hulking knight, and with only a
troubadour to turn to for help! No wonder she needed my assistance. Certainly
the troubadour didn't look as if he'd be
much use if it were to come to any
rough stuff, and he probably didn't have

two brass coins to call his own. My heart went out to the young lovers.

Life could be complicated and difficult, all right.

The song finished, and Duke Wolfhound climbed noisily to his feet, a brimming goblet raised high.

"Sir knights, one and all!" he bellowed. "A toast to our semifinalists! May the best man win!"

"May the best man win!" the crowd roared back.

The matron tapped me on the arm. "I have so enjoyed our little chat," she said. "Good luck tomorrow, sir knight."

I acknowledged her words with a smile and a nod. But I knew that the only luck I'd have was what old Wolfhound would allow me.

FOUR

As the sun reached its highest point in the sky, Jed and I made our way across the tournament field. I could tell by the way he tossed his head and pawed the ground that he was impatient to get underway. As for me, it was another story. I felt lousy! My limbs were heavy, my chest ached, and my head felt as if it had been stuffed with goose down.

The trouble was, I was exhausted. I hadn't slept a wink all night. I just couldn't stop thinking about the fix I was in.

Should I throw the joust, as Duke Wolfhound wanted, and walk away with a heavy purse? Or should I fight fair and save her ladyship, but risk a heavy beating from Wolfhound's thugs? My head said one thing, my heart said another, and I lay awake all night trying to choose. The early morning light was streaming in through the holes of my moth-eaten tent before I decided at last what to do.

I wasn't proud of my decision, I can tell you. It went against every knightly fiber of my body. But though I hated to do it, there was nothing else for it. I would go down to Hengist.

Of course, I'd make it look good. I'd flip from Jed's back and, taking care to cushion my fall, land on the ground in a clatter of armor and a cloud of dust, but then stay down. . . .

Afterward I'd collect my promised gold from Duke Wolfhound and tell him to let her ladyship go, or I'd report him to the herald and bring his tournament-rigging days to an end. And if Hengist were to have a problem with that, we could have a nice little chat about it, away from the tournament field. I also decided that I'd give her ladyship half the gold so that she and the troubadour could travel far away and live happily ever after.

As plans went, it wasn't great; the herald might side with the duke, Hengist might prove to be a bit of a handful, and her ladyship might end up at the top of a tall tower with no staircase. But under the circumstances it was the best I could come up with.

Just then a trumpet sounded loudly, and I looked round to see the herald waddling to the center of the field. The first joust was about to begin.

"At the south end, in wed and white stwipes," the herald proclaimed, "I give you bwave Sir Walph of Mountjoy!"

The crowd cheered.

"At the north end," the herald continued,

"dwessed in blue, the . . . errm . . . the Blue Knight!"

The cheers grew louder. Everyone loves an underdog.

The herald raised his arms. The crowd fell silent. All eyes turned toward her ladyship, who rose to her feet and let a glittering handkerchief flutter down over the balcony. It landed on the grass.

The herald inspected it. "Let the field-of-gold joust commence!" he cried.

At the second trumpet blast the Rich Kid spurred his black warhorse viciously. The animal sprang forward, its ears flat back, its muzzle foaming, the whites of its eyes glinting wildly as it tossed its head. It looked like a creature possessed.

Glancing over at the duke, I noticed the raven-haired handmaid standing behind her ladyship, her dark, glaring eyes fixed on the horse and rider.

At the other end of the field, I saw the Blue Knight urging his bony-looking nag forward. I shook my head. Whoever the Blue Knight was, he certainly wasn't a natural jouster. He rode like an east-country bumpkin, and he couldn't hold his lance steady if his life depended on it. And the way it was looking, it just might, because the Rich Kid had gotten into his stride now.

Keeping the warhorse on target with a tight rein, the Rich Kid leveled his lance and brought his opponent into his sights.

It was a lovely move, one even I would have been proud to perform. The Blue Knight didn't stand a chance.

At least, that was what I thought. But

at that moment an extraordinary thing happened. Just as the two knights were about to clash, the black warhorse let out a terrible whinnying screech, arched its back, and crashed headlong into the tournament turf, pitching the Rich Kid high up in the air . . . and onto the Blue Knight's wavering lance.

There was a bone-shattering crunch, the splintering of wood, and a turf-shuddering crash as the Rich Kid hit the ground. He didn't move. The herald strode across the field and poked the crumpled body with his toe.

"Victowy!" he cried and raised his arm. "The Blue Knight will go through to the final."

The crowd seemed confused. Only a couple of halfhearted cheers rose above the gathering murmur. No one could quite believe what they'd seen. For a healthy warhorse simply to collapse like that was unheard of.

The Rich Kid's four squires rushed forward and fussed about their master.

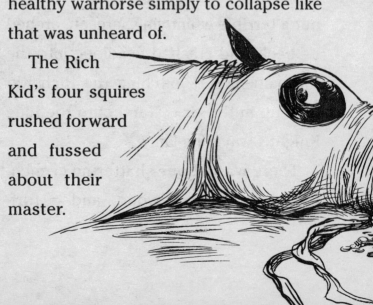

I was more concerned about the stricken warhorse. Dismounting, I strode over and knelt down beside it. The poor creature whimpered, one wild eye staring back at me. There was blood at its mouth, and its front legs were broken.

"There, there, boy," I said. There was nothing I could do.

I looked up to see a man-at-arms approaching with a crossbow. I knew that a bolt through the temple was the kindest thing, but I still couldn't watch. I turned away.

"Come, come, sir knight, it is time," came a familiar voice, and I felt old Pudding Head tugging at my arm.

"Sad that the horse must be put down," he said, "but these things happen."

I nodded. He was right, of course. As he led me away, I noticed the raven-haired handmaid, her eyes boring into mine. I looked away, shocked by the thin smile playing on her lips.

"Huwwy up," said the herald impatiently. "The joust must commence without further delay."

I climbed back onto Jed's back and took my place at the south end of the tournament field.

We waited as the warhorse was dragged off and the Rich Kid—moaning softly now—was stretchered away by his four squires. A ripple of anticipation ran through the crowd. I nodded to those who were cheering me on and raised my head proudly. I might as well enjoy those cheers while they lasted.

I, a free lance, had made it to the semifinals of a major castle tournament. It was only a shame that, on the second tilt, I would have to go down as hard as the Rich Kid before me—and the cheers would turn to boos when the crowd realized that the favorite they'd bet so much on was not getting up.

At the other end of the field Hengist had mounted his stallion. Clad in his dull gray armor, he cut an impressive figure—but was too slow and plodding to be a great jouster. At least, that was what I hoped.

As the trumpet sounded, the herald

stepped forward. "At the north end we have Sir Hengist of the Western Marches."

There were boos amid the cheers as the crowd greeted the local boy.

"At the south end," the herald continued, "Sir . . . um . . . Fwee Lance."

For a second time that afternoon all eyes fell on her ladyship, who climbed to her feet and held the handkerchief high. As our eyes met, a smile fluttered uncertainly across her face. I lowered my visor.

The handkerchief fell.

"Let the field-of-gold joust commence!" cried the herald.

With a loud snort, Hengist spurred his horse. I twitched Jed's reins, and he was off. Beneath me I could feel his pounding hooves gathering speed. How he loved

the tourna-
ments—the
charged air in
his nostrils,
the boiling
blood cours-
ing through
his body.

I raised my
shield, fixed
my sights on
Hengist,
and leveled

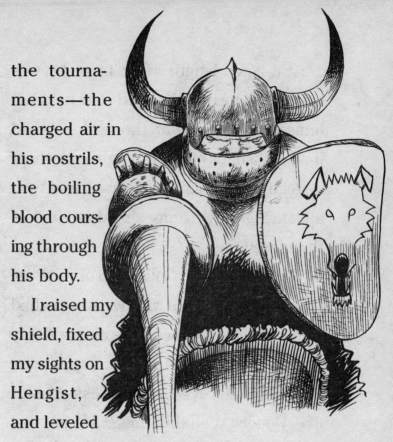

my lance. All brawn and no brain, the oaf
was lumbering toward me, bouncing
about in his saddle like a cider barrow in
an ox cart. His great, heavy armor was
doing him no favors either, pitching him
this way and that.

At a lance length away, I saw he was leaning so heavily forward that he'd left himself wide open at the neck. I could have finished him off there and then. Instead, I turned my lance away and took a glancing blow to my shield as Hengist thundered past.

The crowd gave a loud gasp of surprise.

On the second joust, as we approached each other, I deliberately dropped my shoulder and raised my shield, offering a target that even a hopeless jouster like Hengist couldn't miss. Urging Jed on, I shifted my lance round so that it would glance harmlessly off Hengist's armor. Then, at the last possible moment, I slipped my feet from the stirrups and got ready for the heavy blow that I knew was about to come.

I wasn't disappointed. The air abruptly filled with the sound of shattering wood and a desperate cry from the crowd as Hengist's lance struck the top of my breastplate, and I shot from the saddle like a speared moat-fish.

I hit the ground hard and rolled over and over, clattering like a brewer's barrel on cobblestones. If I had to go down, the least I

could do was put on a show. I came to rest just near the grandstand—a nice touch, I thought—and lay there, stock-still.

It was all over.

Through my visor I glimpsed the shocked face of her ladyship looking down at me miserably, the color drained from her cheeks. Beside her, Duke Wolfhound was smiling unpleasantly. He knew he'd won.

Just then I became aware of a fierce, stabbing pain in my shoulder where Hengist's lance had struck. I'd felt the blow of a blunted tournament lance many times before—a dull, bruising ache. But this was different. I put my hand to my shoulder and was shocked to feel the end of a shattered lance shaft.

I pulled myself up—to the gasps and

cries of the crowd, who had already written me off—and tugged at the length of splintered wood. I found myself holding the pointed iron tip of a war lance.

I'd been taken for a fool! A total sap! The duke had never intended to pay me for throwing the joust at all. He'd merely wanted me off my guard so that his great hulking henchman could finish me off for good. If I hadn't ridden

the blow so well, I'd be dead now.

A red mist descended. I was gripped by a murderous rage.

I jumped to my feet, and as I drew my sword, the crowd gave a thunderous roar.

Hengist was lumbering toward me, his own broadsword gripped in a great ham of a hand. I threw myself at him, meeting his lunging uppercut with a high parry.

Our swords clashed, and I felt as if a red-hot poker were boring into my shoulder. With a roar of pain, I dummied a high sword cut to his right, though swung low instead. It was an old trick, but one that caught Hengist totally off guard. As my broadsword sliced into the back of his knees, he crashed to the ground, bellowing like a wounded bear.

I stood over him, my sword raised

high, about to bring it crashing down, when I felt a hand on my shoulder. It was the herald.

"There seems to have been a slight mix-up with the lances," he said out of the corner of his mouth while smiling for the benefit of the cheering crowd. "Most unfortunate, but we don't want it to get out of hand, do we?"

The red mist was lifting, and I suddenly felt very tired.

"After all," the herald was saying, "this is a field of gold, not a field of blood, wemember."

I lowered my sword. My head was swimming, and my shoulder hurt more than ever.

"My lords, ladies, and gentlemen," the herald announced loudly, "Fwee Lance is thwough to the final!"

FIVE

Her ladyship was staring down at me, her eyes brimming with tears of happiness and thanks. Beside her, Duke Wolfhound's face told a different story. With his eyes blazing and his fangs bared, he looked like a cornered dog in a bear pit.

He clicked his fingers, and two beefy henchmen appeared at his side. At his whispered command they clattered down the grandstand steps and lumbered onto the tournament field, their broadswords drawn.

Things were not looking good.

Then something surprising happened. As the two goons approached, I heard a rising swell of noise behind me and turned to see a crowd of joyful spectators burst through the rope fence. Jostling Duke Wolfhound's goons aside, they seized me, hoisted me up onto their shoulders, and carried me off, chanting my name loudly as they went.

"Free Lance! Free Lance!"

It was little wonder I was so popular, I realized, for most of the crowd had bet on me and were celebrating collecting their winnings. Everyone was laughing and cheering and clapping me on the back. Everyone, that is, except Duke Wolfhound.

From my vantage point I could see him scowling at me. With a wave of his hand, he called off his henchmen. There was nothing any of them could do. At least, not for now.

But I knew the matter wouldn't stop there. Duke

Wolfhound wasn't the sort to forgive and forget. The cold, calculating look on his face told me it wasn't his pride that was hurting him—it was his purse.

The crowd carried me round the tournament field three times, before trooping me back to my tent. Wormrick came across to greet me.

"Well done, sir!" he said. "I knew you could . . ." He gasped. "Sir!" he exclaimed. "You're bleeding!"

In all the excitement I'd clean forgotten about my injury. Suddenly it all came flooding back. The lance blow. The pain. The blood . . . I looked down at my breastplate. It was dripping with the stuff.

I'm not usually the squeamish type. I've seen my fair share of brave knights cut down on the battlefield, but this was different. This was my blood—and lots of it! Wormrick's face swam before my eyes, and my head suddenly felt heavier than a lead weight.

A black sea opened up before me— and I dived straight in.

I opened my eyes and tried to focus them. Slowly the blurred shapes in front of me sharpened into a smiling mouth and two emerald-green eyes.

"You're awake," her ladyship said, her voice breaking with relief. "Thank goodness. I was beginning to fear the worst."

"Your ladyship," I said, sitting up and immediately wishing I hadn't. A burning pain bore through my shoulder like a newly forged nail.

"Easy now," she said. "Lie back again, sweet sir knight. Let me finish dressing your wound."

I did as I was told, and sank back into the downy pillows and soft mattress. It was like floating on a cloud.

"Where am I?" I asked.

"The servants' quarters in the castle," she said as she applied a thick, green ointment to my shoulder. The effect was so great, I almost expected to hear the hiss of steam as the wound cooled. "I had you brought here because it wasn't safe for you to return to your tent. My uncle's henchmen are looking for you."

I nodded grimly.

"But you have done me a great service, sir knight," she continued, "and I want to do everything I can to ensure you come to no harm." She was bandaging me up as she spoke. "Thankfully, your injuries are not too bad, but you must rest."

"Rest!" I exclaimed. "But the tournament . . . the final!"

"That's not till tomorrow," said her ladyship firmly. "So be a good knight, lie back, and let the ointment take effect. Besides," she added, "there are others far worse off than you." A smile plucked at the corners of her mouth. "Sir Hengist, for one," she said. "My uncle's washed his hands of him and sent him packing."

"So the wedding's off," I said, smiling.

"Good job I didn't shell out any money for a wedding present."

"You've done more than enough for me already," she replied, returning my smile as she knotted the ends of the bandage underneath my arm. "Thanks to you, my plans are complete. Tomorrow, when the tournament is over, I shall leave my uncle's castle forever."

"I wish you luck, your ladyship," I said. "It can be a harsh world beyond a castle's walls."

"Luck has nothing to do with it," she said, her green eyes gleaming with excitement. "My beloved has arranged everything. He has two fine, strong horses waiting and has bribed the castle gatekeeper with his last two gold crowns. It might be a harsh world as you say, but with him at my side I can face anything." She smiled and planted a kiss on my forehead. "And it's all thanks to you, sweet sir knight."

"Don't mention it," I said, lying back against the soft pillows, the touch of her lips lingering on my forehead.

Her ladyship straightened the blankets. "All done," she announced. "Now, I must go and prepare myself for this evening's banquet. It wouldn't do to turn up late. My uncle mustn't suspect a thing." She squeezed my hand warmly. "Rest here, sir knight, until you're feeling completely recovered."

With that, she turned and skipped from the room, seemingly without a care in the world. I hoped it would all work out for her. I'd done all I could. Now it was up to that troubadour of hers. I could only pray, for both their sakes, that he was up to the task. I had more than enough cares of my own right now.

Despite her ladyship's parting words,

I could not risk remaining in bed a moment longer—however comfortable it might be. If the duke's henchmen were to find my tent empty, I knew they would try to get to me through Jed or Wormrick. I had to get back to them and make sure they were all right.

Slipping reluctantly from beneath the warm bedcover, I shivered in my patched leggings and bare feet and looked round the room for the rest of my clothes. I only hoped her ladyship hadn't sent them to the castle laundry.

At the end of the room stood a three-paneled wooden screen, behind which I could see the edge of a mirror and the corner of a chair sticking out. With a bit of luck, I'd find my missing clothes there as well.

I padded across the floor and looked. And there they were, all folded up neatly on the chair. It was the first bit of good luck I'd had all day. I quickly slipped the jerkin over my head, secured the sword around my waist, and had just sat down to pull on my boots when I heard someone entering the room.

I froze. Had one of the duke's henchmen found me after all?

Gripping my sword, I leaned slowly forward in the chair and peered round the edge of the screen. There was someone in the room. But it was no guard. Instead I found

myself looking at her ladyship's raven-haired handmaid. She had something in her hand—a small vial or jar—and was unstoppering it as she made her way across the room.

The next moment, finding my bed empty, she stamped her foot petulantly and her eyes darted furi-ously around the room. There was something about her dark look that made me decide not to give

myself away. I shrank back into the shadows behind the screen and waited.

The next moment there came a voice.

"So," it said, "looks like her ladyship's
guest has flown the coop." I edged

myself forward and peered through a hinged gap in the screen to see the troubadour, of all people, striding into the room. "And before you had a chance to weave your magic on him," he said. "How very unfortunate."

The handmaid tossed her black hair and narrowed her eyes. "You concentrate on your job," she said icily. "I'll concentrate on mine."

"Oh, don't you worry about me," said the troubadour, strumming lightly on his lute as he sat himself down on the bed and put his feet up. "You keep

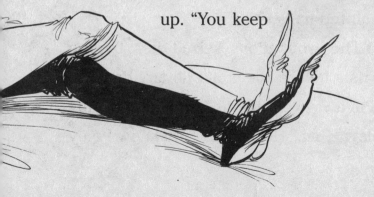

knocking them down, and I'll keep taking the glory."

The handmaid's hands flew to her hips. "If that were all you were doing, it would be fine," she said angrily. "But I swear you're turning into her ladyship's lapdog. Trailing after her the whole time, tongue hanging out . . ."

The troubadour threw back his head and laughed. Then, laying his lute aside, he jumped to his feet and went to take the handmaid in his arms.

"Get off me!" she shrieked, and scratched at his face with her sharp, pointed nails.

The troubadour seized her by the wrists before she could do any damage. "Put away your talons," he said. "I'm only playacting." He smiled. "You know I only

have eyes for you, my raven-haired sorceress."

I saw the handmaid visibly soften. "I can never stay angry with you for long," she said quietly, and shuddered. "It's this place. The sooner we leave, the better."

The troubadour nodded. "It's a great shame that brave Free Lance is not here," he said thoughtfully. "It would have made things so much easier."

"It doesn't matter. I'll take care of Free Lance," she said, hitching up her long gown and hurrying to the door. "And just make sure you're not too busy 'play-acting' to take advantage of it when I do," she called back.

The troubadour sat himself back down on the bed and started strumming the lute, and singing in that rich, honeyed voice of his that so thrilled all the ladies.

"My love has eyes of emerald green . . ." He paused and chuckled. "Or should that be, my love has hair of raven black . . . ?"

All at once, he stopped playing, jumped to his feet, and tucked his lute under his arm. "Best be off," he said. "After all, a banquet isn't a banquet without a troubadour."

As he left the room, I pulled my boots on at last, buckled up my breastplate, and emerged from behind the screen. My shoulder ached, but it was the least of my worries. I didn't know what the troubadour and the handmaid were up to, but it seemed to involve yours truly. One thing was certain— if her ladyship thought she could rely on the troubadour, she was making a big mistake. I hated to be the one to break the bad news, but for the time being, at least, it could wait.

Right now I had to get to Wormrick and Jed. In the meantime her ladyship could enjoy

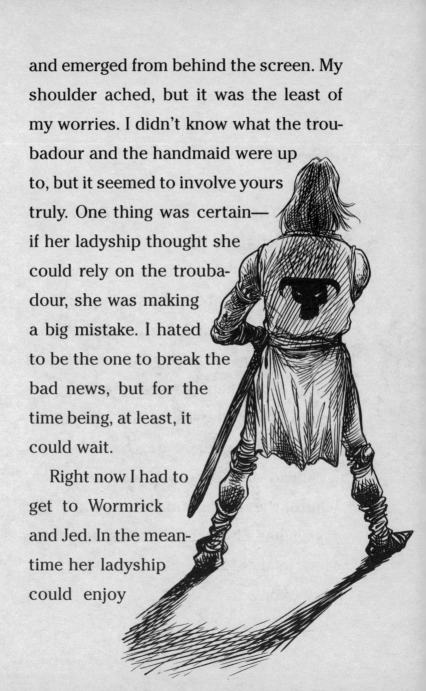

what she thought was her last banquet—
the finalists' banquet.

Not that you'd catch me in that viper's
den—not after the day I'd just had. No, I
planned to be as mysterious as the Blue
Knight. There would be two empty seats
at the high table that evening.

Using the old tossed-stone trick to dis-
tract the guard at the gate, I slipped away
from the castle and darted off between
the collection of costly tents and elegant
marquees. I kept to the shadows, my
head down and eyes on the lookout for
any sign of danger.

Ahead of me the rocky thistle patch,
where the more modest knights like
myself had pitched their tents, came into
view. I saw at once that something was
very wrong.

SIX

As I approached, I spotted two burly oafs dressed in Duke Wolfhound's colors, standing outside my tent, flaming torches in their hands. They were clearly waiting for someone, and it didn't take a genius to work out who.

The larger of the two, a powerfully built goon with cropped red hair, noticed me. An ugly smile spread across his blotchy face.

"Just the knight we've been looking

for," he sneered, and nudged his companion, a pasty-faced oaf with a scar down one cheek.

Scarface smiled. "That's right," he agreed. "You see, there's been an unfortunate accident."

"Accident?" I said.

"Yes, sir knight," said Scarface. "A fire." He lowered the torch and held it to the tent flap. With a crackle and a puff of smoke, a sheet of blazing yellow leaped up the side of my tent.

"Tut-tut," said Ginger, drawing a great cudgel from his belt. "First your tent accidentally burns down, and then you have a nasty fall."

"I do?" I said, my hand gripping the handle of my sword.

"That's right," said Scarface. "A very nasty fall. Two broken legs, I believe."

I drew my sword as Ginger lunged. The heavy cudgel whistled past my ear. He wasn't trying to break my legs—it was a crushed skull he was after.

I stepped to one side and drove the handle of my sword hard into the pit of his stomach. As he lurched forward, I gave him a crushing blow to the back of the head. The great oaf crashed to the ground.

"Sweet dreams," I muttered.

One down, one to go. I spun round

to see Scarface, a mace raised above his head, about to brain me. I swung my sword in a low, slashing cut that drew a red line across the blue and white quarters on his chest. It was just a flesh wound, but it did the trick.

Scarface dropped his weapon and let out a long, loud squeal, like a greased runt at a pig-catching contest. I took a step forward, but he'd clearly had enough. Turning on his heels, he fled without a backward glance.

I sheathed my sword and took stock. My tent was now fully ablaze, the fire devouring the tent cloth like a plague of fiery moths.

Suddenly—with a loud *whumpph!*—the whole lot collapsed.

Practically everything I owned had been in that tent, but I didn't care about that. No, what was really on my mind was the fate of Wormrick and Jed.

I dashed off to the stables, praying I'd find them both there, safe and sound.

I elbowed my way through the crowd of knights and squires that had gathered to watch the fire, and burst in through the stable doors.

"Wormrick!" I bellowed. "Wormrick!"

Ahead of me there came a soft rustle from one of the far stalls, and a freckled face peered up at me from the straw.

"Oh, sir," Wormick said as he climbed to his feet. "I've been so worried. The duke sent a couple of his men to find you."

"I know," I said, smiling. "They gave me quite a warm reception."

"I grabbed what I could and came here," Wormrick went on. "First thing I did was to disguise Jed. That patched surcoat of his is a bit of a giveaway. So I swapped it over, hid myself, and waited. I didn't know what else to do."

"You did well, Wormrick," I said. "I'm proud of you."

Just then I felt hot breath on the back of my neck. I turned and saw Jed standing beside me, dressed in a black-and-silver surcoat. I recognized it at once. It had belonged to the Rich Kid's warhorse.

Maybe Jed sensed that he was draped in the surcoat of a dead horse. Maybe the commotion outside had unnerved him. Whatever it was, he was certainly not his usual self, pawing at the ground, rolling his eyes, and gnashing at the bit.

"It's all right, Jed," I said, patting him on his neck. "Everything's all right."

Soon he was snorting down his nose into my face and licking at the saltiness in my palms as if nothing at all had ever been the matter. Outside, the commotion got suddenly louder. Jeers and whistles rose up above loud, angry voices.

"Wait here, Wormrick," I said. "I think our friends are back. Guard Jed. And make sure no one touches him."

I drew my sword a second time, headed for the stable doors, and strode outside. A semicircle of faces greeted me, each one uglier than the last. Ginger and Scarface were among them and, in the middle of the line, Duke Wolfhound himself. As our gazes met, his eyes narrowed menacingly.

"I thought we had a deal, sir knight," he hissed. He looked round and addressed his henchmen. "It seems that these days, knights aren't to be trusted—but then, what can you expect from a free lance?"

"It takes two to honor a deal," I replied calmly. "You didn't mention the war lance when we made our little agreement," I said, my shoulder throbbing at the memory.

"Ah yes, that," said Duke Wolfhound. "I'm afraid Hengist got a little over-enthusiastic. He's no longer in my employ.

And neither," he added pointedly, "are you. Guards!" he bellowed. "Seize him!"

As one, the burly oafs advanced toward me, their cudgels and maces swinging. Things weren't looking good. My throbbing shoulder was about to become the least of my worries.

"Stop wight there!" cried an outraged voice.

It was the herald, buttoning up his tabard as he hurried toward us. His eyes fell upon Duke Wolfhound.

"So this is where you've got to, Your Gwace," he said. "Shouldn't you be at the banquet attending to your guests?"

"Yes, yes," said the duke. "I have a small matter to clear up here first, herald," he said. "I shan't be long."

The herald pursed his lips. "Your Gwace," he said, "if you have a pwoblem with one of your knights, it is usual to consult the hewald."

Duke Wolfhound looked flustered.

"I . . . I didn't think . . ." he began.

"That is the twouble," said the herald sharply. "You didn't think!"

He stepped forward. "I am the hewald. I weport diwectly to the Gwand Tournament Council. If they were to hear of this, then your status as the host of a gwand tournament might well be at wisk."

"But . . . but . . ." the duke began.

"Never mind your 'buts,'" said the herald. "There have been a number of complaints at this tournament alweady. Horses behaving oddly. Stwangely large bets placed on complete outsiders," he continued, staring pointedly at Duke Wolfhound. "And it has also come to my notice that a tent has been burned down."

Shamefaced, Ginger and Scarface looked down at their boots.

"And now I find a knight about to be attacked," he cried. "I won't have it! Not at a tournament of which I am the hewald! Call off your men, Your Gwace, or the next tournament you'll host will be of the village-gween vawiety! I twust I make myself clear."

Duke Wolfhound scowled. "Yes," he snarled, and snapped his fingers.

His henchmen backed off, and the whole lot of them slunk away. I turned to the herald. "Thank you," I said.

"Don't thank me, Fwee Lance," he replied sharply. "Knights like you attwact twouble wherever they go. You don't belong in a major tournament. But since you're here, it is my duty to make sure the wules are followed to the letter!"

With that, he turned on his heels and strode off. I watched him go. A stickler for the rules he might be, but that was exactly the type I needed to make it to the end of the tournament in one piece. After that, however, I'd be on my own.

I went back to the stables. Despite the chill wind that had picked up outside, it was warm inside the stable, and the straw smelled sweet and inviting. I slumped down, curled up, and closed my eyes. . . . The next thing I knew, Wormrick was shaking me by the shoulders.

"I've rubbed down Jed and polished your armor, sir," he was saying. "And her ladyship has sent a tray of quail's eggs from the castle kitchens for your breakfast."

Duke Wolfhound hadn't finished with me yet. I knew I'd need more than quail's eggs to see me through the long day ahead.

I had yet to discover just how long that day would be.

SEVEN

A trumpet blast echoed round the soggy tournament field. The excited clamor of the crowd died down, and all eyes fell on the herald, who strode forward, his boots sinking into the mud with every step. The heavy morning rain had given way to a persistent drizzle, and I was wet and cold.

At the far end of the field I saw the Blue Knight climbing awkwardly into the saddle. Beneath me Jed trembled.

"What's up, boy?" I whispered. Usually

the trumpet blast would have him pawing the ground and chomping at the bit, but not today. No, today Jed was lethargic yet nervy, and had hardly touched his breakfast, even though Wormrick had served him up the finest oat mash the castle had to offer.

"Everything all right, sir?" came a voice, and I turned to see Wormrick standing beside us, my lance in his hands.

"I'm worried about Jed," I told him. "Are you sure none of the duke's men have gotten to him?"

"They couldn't have, sir. I was with him all evening. I'd have noticed any funny business." He paused. "Mind you, there was one thing . . ."

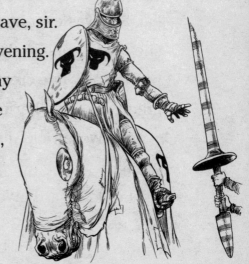

"Yes?" I said.

"No, it's nothing, sir."

"Tell me, Wormrick."

"Well," he said, his brow furrowing. "It was that lady."

"What lady?"

"Her ladyship's handmaid," he said. "You know, the one with the black hair."

"What about her?" I asked.

"It's just that when I first got to the stables, she was there. With Jed. Patting him, she was, and whispering into his ear. She was ever so gentle, though. Said she loved horses, sir, and that Jed was a particularly fine creature," he added. "So I didn't see any harm in it, sir."

"No, Wormrick," I said. "I'm sure there wasn't."

"Look," said Wormrick, pointing.

"There she is now, sir, staring at Jed. Can't keep her eyes off him."

I turned, looked up at the raised grandstand, and straight into the poisonous gaze of the raven-haired handmaid. A thin smile danced on her lips.

I shivered. I had a bad feeling about this, a really bad feeling.

In front of her sat her ladyship, next to Duke Wolfhound. A second trumpet blast echoed round the field, and her ladyship arose. Her face was as white as a sheet, and she was trembling violently.

The Blue Knight had taken his lance from his squire and was holding it like a matron with a walking stick.

The herald raised

his hand. "Ladies and gentlemen," he cried. "The gwand final!"

A loud cheer went up. The herald turned toward the grandstand. "If your ladyship would be so kind."

Ashen-faced, her ladyship fumbled with the silken purse in her hands. Scowling, the duke nudged her roughly, and I saw him raise his hand to conceal the words he hissed at her.

She nodded. The next moment, she dipped into the purse and raised her arm high in the air. Instead of the gold handkerchief I had expected, there was a bloodred handkerchief clasped in her hand.

The crowd gasped as one. Even the herald looked shocked.

"Are you quite sure, your ladyship?" he asked.

"Of course she's sure," Duke Wolfhound answered for her. "As Queen of the Tournament Field, she has every right, I think you'll find."

He rested his hand heavily on her shoulder. "Release it," he snarled.

Tears streaming down her cheeks, her ladyship let the handkerchief drop. It fluttered to the ground like a wounded sparrow. The herald stepped forward.

"A field-of-blood joust," he announced, his voice quavering. "A fight to the death."

I shook my head. So this was what Duke Wolfhound had planned. It was clever. Devilishly clever. If the Blue Knight were to kill me, then the duke would have

117

gotten his revenge. If, on the other hand, I were to beat the Blue Knight, then I'd have to kill him to claim the champion's prize. Wolfhound clearly didn't think I had the guts to do it, which meant he wouldn't have to pay out. Either way, in his twisted mind, he ended up winning.

Life in the majors! I thought with a shudder. It might look glamorous from the outside, but inside it was rotten.

"Let the field-of-blood joust commence!" the herald cried.

I turned to Wormrick. "May as well get this over with," I said. "Wish me luck!"

The trumpet sounded a third time, and I twitched Jed's reins. He didn't move. I could feel the raven-haired handmaid's gaze on us from the grandstand, like a hawk eyeing its prey.

"Come on, Jed," I urged. "Don't let me down, not now. . . ."

All at once, Jed lurched forward and immediately picked up speed, galloping over the spongy ground. The Blue Knight hurtled toward me, flapping about like a fat abbot on a donkey, his lance all over the place. I couldn't miss.

I really hated to do this to him, whoever he was, but I had no choice. It was him

or me. I lowered my lance into position.

Suddenly beneath me I felt a tremendous spasm run through Jed's body from head to tail. Arching his back, he crashed into the sodden field, sending me flying through the air. The ground rushed up to meet me. The next thing I knew, there was a roaring noise in my ears and I was seeing stars.

There was mud everywhere—in my eyes, my mouth. I spat out the foul-tasting filth as I scrambled to my feet.

From behind me came the pounding of hooves.

I lurched round.

The Blue Knight was bearing down on me, a great studded

mace in his hand. Before I could react, the mace struck me, and I went down for a second time.

I became aware of the crowd scream-ing and shouting and baying for blood. I rolled over. The Blue Knight had dismounted. His mace lay discarded behind him. In his hands was a heavy-looking broadsword, which hissed through the air as he approached to finish me off.

There was blood in my mouth, the sun in my eyes . . . I never imagined that it would end like this.

The Blue Knight stood over me and raised his sword above his head, ready to plunge it into my heart. He was so close I could see his blue eyes twinkling from behind his visor. Too close . . .

With every last ounce of strength, I kicked and took the knight's legs out from under him.

It was his turn to come crashing to the ground. I was on my feet and on him in an instant, my sword at his throat.

The crowd roared with delight. . . . *To the death . . . to the death*—the herald's words echoed inside my head.

Just then I heard an unspeakable screech from the grandstand. I looked round to see the raven-haired handmaid racing toward me, her talons drawn, her teeth bared, and her thick, black hair streaming back behind her.

"No!" she screamed. *"No!"*

Two men-at-arms leaped forward and pulled her back.

"No! No!" she cried. "I won't let you kill him!"

A murmur went round the crowd.

I glanced up at Duke Wolfhound. An evil sneer played on his lips.

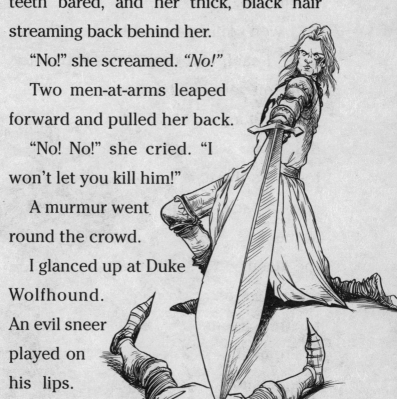

"It's a field of blood, Free Lance!" He smiled, his fangs glinting. "You're going to have to kill him if you want your money."

With a nod, the herald confirmed that the duke was right. "Wules are wules," he murmured.

"I won't kill a man without seeing his face," I said, and drew my sword back. "Take off your helmet."

The Blue Knight did as he was told. And there, staring back at me, was the handsome face of the troubadour.

From the grandstand

her ladyship gave a scream and jumped up from her seat.

"What are you waiting for, sir knight?" the troubadour said bitterly. "Go on. Finish me off . . ."

"No! No!" screeched the handmaid, struggling with her captors. "Don't listen to him, Free Lance. He is no knight— anybody can see that. He's just a poor troubadour. He doesn't deserve to die. It was I who bewitched your horse and all the others, so that he would win the tournament. And then we'd be rich enough to be married and give up this wandering life. . . ."

"Married? But he loves me!" her ladyship cried from the grandstand.

"Loves you?" The handmaid glared at her ladyship. "He could never love a pampered princess like you. You were just a plaything. He told me so."

Her ladyship stared imploringly at the troubadour. A cruel smile played on his lips.

"It was fun while it lasted," he said. "But now it's over. What are you waiting for, Free Lance?"

"You heard the scum," Duke Wolfhound sneered. "He's only a troubadour. He won't be missed." He laughed when I did not move. "Just as I suspected. Our brave Free Lance here hasn't the stomach for a field of blood. My money's safe!"

The herald stepped forward. "It is unfortunate," he said, "but there is nothing I can do. A field of blood is a field of blood. Of course, there will be an investigation afterward, but that won't help our fwiend now. Either finish him off, Fwee Lance, or lose the purse."

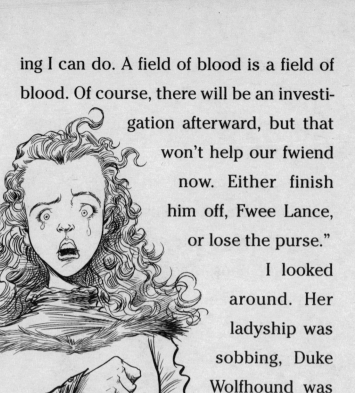

I looked around. Her ladyship was sobbing, Duke Wolfhound was sneering, and the handmaid was wringing her hands. As for the troubadour, he was glaring at me defiantly.

"Kill! Kill!" cried a couple of voices from

the crowd, and soon the whole lot of them were chanting loudly. "Kill! Kill! Kill!"

I raised my sword . . . and returned it to its sheath.

I glanced around at the jeering faces as the chanting abruptly gave way to cat-calls and boos. And at that moment I knew I'd had it with the major tourna-ments. From now on I'd stick to the manor-house circuit and the occasional village green.

"You all disgust me," I said, spitting on the ground as I turned and walked away from the tournament field.

Jed came trotting up to me as if nothing had happened, with Wormrick running behind him. It was good to see them. I couldn't wait to get away from the place. But first, there was one last thing I had to do.

"Thank you, thank you, brave sir knight," her ladyship said, her emerald-green eyes sparkling brightly. "I don't know how I can ever repay you."

"I'm just glad to have been of help," I said.

"Oh, you have," she cried. "Without you, I would never have gotten out of the clutches of my wicked uncle." She looked around. "And I'm sure I'll be happy here. They're good people."

I nodded. She was right. They might not be able to joust, but the east-country noblemen had kind hearts.

We were standing in front of the manor house of one of her distant cousins, and as she waved good-bye, I knew that I'd be leaving her in good hands. And with the thirty gold pieces Duke Wolfhound had first bribed me with, she'd be able to hire a more reliable handmaid than the last one.

The raven-haired sorceress had been drummed out of town with that troubadour boyfriend of hers. As for Duke Wolfhound, he'd saved the prize money, and I'd talked the herald out of reporting him to the Grand Tournament Council. In return the duke had let her ladyship go. If he was ashamed of making her drop the red handkerchief, he showed no sign of it.

I sighed. I might not have taken the winner's purse, but at least I had no blood on my hands. And besides, one good thing had come out of the whole escapade: a faithful squire.

"Where to now, sir?" Wormrick asked as we galloped off.

"I've no idea," I replied.

"Sir?" said Wormrick, looking confused.

"You are a squire to a free lance now, Wormrick," I said. "I can't promise you riches, or soft beds, or warm hearths, but there's one thing I can give you in plenty."

"What's that?" asked Wormrick, his voice deep and steady.

"Adventure," I said.

AND HERE'S
A BIT OF THE ACTION
FROM FREE LANCE'S
NEXT ADVENTURE:

DRAGON'S
HOARD
A KNIGHT'S STORY 3

Being bodyguard to a rich merchant was a nice little earner for a knight down on his luck. At least that's what I'd thought three weeks earlier, when I was offered this job. I should have known it wasn't going to be that simple. It never is.

"There are many dangers along the way," he said, his voice hushed, his eyes narrowed. "Brigands. Wolves. And possibly worse . . ."

We set off bright and early in the morning. And as the sun rose higher, a low mist gave way to a bright, cloudless sky. The land grew drier and more desolate. Large scavenger birds, with curved beaks and ragged wings, wheeled across the sky as we left the city far behind us.

It became clear soon enough that the merchant was right about our route. There were brigands, though they were easy to spot, hanging around at crossroads and in the hills above mountain passes. Brigands aren't hard to avoid if you scout ahead and keep your eyes peeled, travel during the day and set up a secure camp at night. And the same goes for wolves, only with a good, bright campfire thrown in.

Of course, with a dozen heavily laden mules and the Peacock on his skittish white mare, Jed and I couldn't relax for a moment. Backward and forward we went, to and fro, covering plenty of ground to make sure they all stayed safe. It was certainly tiring. Then again, compared to slaying monstrous hags and surviving blood-drenched tournaments, being a bodyguard to a rich merchant was easy.

A fortnight later we came within a day's ride of our final destination. I could almost feel those fifty pieces of gold jangling in my pocket.

The sun had just slipped down beneath the horizon when I called a halt. The Peacock wasn't happy. He wanted to press on through the night and get back home, which was understandable. Understandable and foolish. Wolves liked nothing better than a night hunt, and we were in typical, wolf country—a rocky, desolate plain, fringed with jagged mountains.

There was a chill wind blowing, which stirred up the dust and whistled between the boulders. It was spooky, but I was far too busy to let it bother me.

I had the mules to secure, Jed to settle, a fire to build, the torches to light, a meal to prepare . . . As ever, the Peacock said little and did even less. Even so I could tell that he wasn't happy. In fact he looked as nervous as a goose in a cook's kitchen. He flapped about anxiously as he tethered his skittish mare, Sherazah, to a rock. He was muttering under his breath and constantly looking over his shoulder.

"Something tells me you're not crazy about my choice of campsite," I said to him later, as I served him up a portion of my Squire's Stew.

He shuddered and pulled his cape around him. "This, my friend," he said, "is an evil place."

"Evil place?" I said.

He nodded. "The Plain of the Dead, it is called," he said.

"Interesting name. Let me guess . . . ," I said, stifling a smile. "Now you're going to tell me why."